About  Illustrator

Name: ....

Age: .... Hometown: ....

The most adventurous thing I've ever done is:

....

....

If I went to outer space, I'd like to see:

....

....

The best thing about planet Earth is:

....

....

Surfing on a Star

COMPENDIUM®

kids™

inspiring possibilities.™

I was playing outside when
I heard a loud whoosh.

I looked up to see
a huge spaceship.

It landed in my yard,
and the door opened.

A strange pilot with
lots of arms greeted me.

I climbed in.

The inside of the spaceship had buttons and lights everywhere.

I pushed the **biggest** button.

The lights flickered, and we zoomed off into outer space!

We started floating around

inside the spaceship.

Then, I took a turn at the steering wheel.

We flew right by a planet with colorful rings around it.

We landed, and there were lots of friendly aliens.

They showed me
how to space surf.

And then they invited us
to stay for lunch!

When it was time to go,
I jumped on a shooting star
and rode it all the way home.

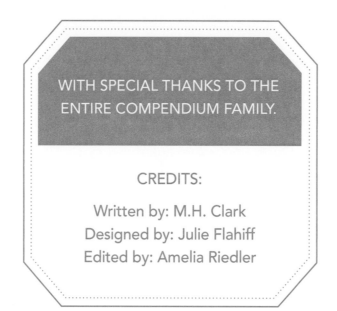

WITH SPECIAL THANKS TO THE
ENTIRE COMPENDIUM FAMILY.

CREDITS:

Written by: M.H. Clark
Designed by: Julie Flahiff
Edited by: Amelia Riedler

ISBN: 978-1-938298-24-0

1st printing. Printed in China with soy inks. A011310001

COMPENDIUM®

kids™

inspiring possibilities.™